W9-CCM-643

Beaver Gets Lost

Ariane Chottin
Adapted by Deborah Kovacs
Illustrations by Marcelle Geneste

Reader's Digest Kids
Pleasantville, N.Y.–Montreal

Once a family of red squirrels lived in a little wood of sturdy oaks beside a bubbling stream. As the young squirrels played on a hollow log one crisp fall afternoon, a little animal with dark brown fur waddled up. "I think I'm lost," he said.

"Don't worry," said Mother Squirrel. "We'll take care of you."

"Hooray," cried all the little squirrels. "We've got a new brother!"

"My name is Josie," said one little squirrel, scrambling down the tree trunk. "What's yours?"

"Clarence," answered the little animal shyly.

At first the squirrel family thought Clarence was a squirrel, too. Only Father Squirrel was puzzled about Clarence's tail. It was flat and covered with black scales, not fluffy and red like the others in the family. But it didn't matter. He and the rest of the squirrel family soon came to love Clarence as one of their own.

One day, Father and Mother Squirrel tried to teach their children how to build a nest. But the young squirrels wouldn't sit still for the lesson. They chased each other up trees and tossed acorns from the branches. Only Clarence paid attention. He listened carefully to every word Father Squirrel said.

"I can't wait to build my own nest!" said Clarence. He got right to work, dragging long branches across the forest to the clearing.

As he worked, Clarence's nest started to look very different from the one Father Squirrel had built. Instead of layering small leaves and twigs in a pile, Clarence stood big sticks upright, leaning one against the other, and used his tail to pat mud in the cracks.

Back and forth he went, dragging bigger and bigger branches past his astonished family.

For days, Clarence kept at his work.
Josie sat up on a branch and watched him.
She wished he would play with her
instead. "When will you be done?" she
asked.

Clarence looked at his nest. "Not for a
long time," he answered. "There's still a
lot of work to do."

The animals in the forest gathered to watch Clarence. "What's he doing?" one squirrel asked Josie.

"He's been building that thing for days," said the weasel.

Josie shook her head. "He never stops," she said. "He just keeps working."

Clarence's nest got bigger and bigger.
Still, he kept building.

"Do you want me to help you?" Josie
asked, hoping he'd be done soon.

"Oh, yes!" said Clarence. "Would you
please help me find more branches to use
while I cut down this tree?"

"Okay," sighed Josie, scampering into
the woods.

That was how Josie found a whole family of animals just like Clarence! They had big front teeth and broad flat tails and they were building a huge nest of sticks.

"Just like Clarence!" Josie cried. "Wait until I tell everybody!"

Josie was out of breath when she finally reached the family oak tree in the forest.

"Clarence! Clarence!" she cried. "I think I found your family down at the river! They're making a nest just like yours!"

"Where, Josie?" cried Clarence. "Please show me!"

"May we come, too?" the young squirrels
begged their parents.

"Why not?" said Mother Squirrel.
Everyone rushed after Josie and Clarence,
who were headed for the riverbank.

Clarence and his mother and father were so happy to see each other again! "How can we ever thank you for taking such good care of our little beaver?" asked his mother.

"Beaver?" laughed Mother Squirrel. "Why, we thought he was a squirrel! But it doesn't matter. Just promise to let Clarence visit us in the woods from time to time. Our family has grown quite fond of him."

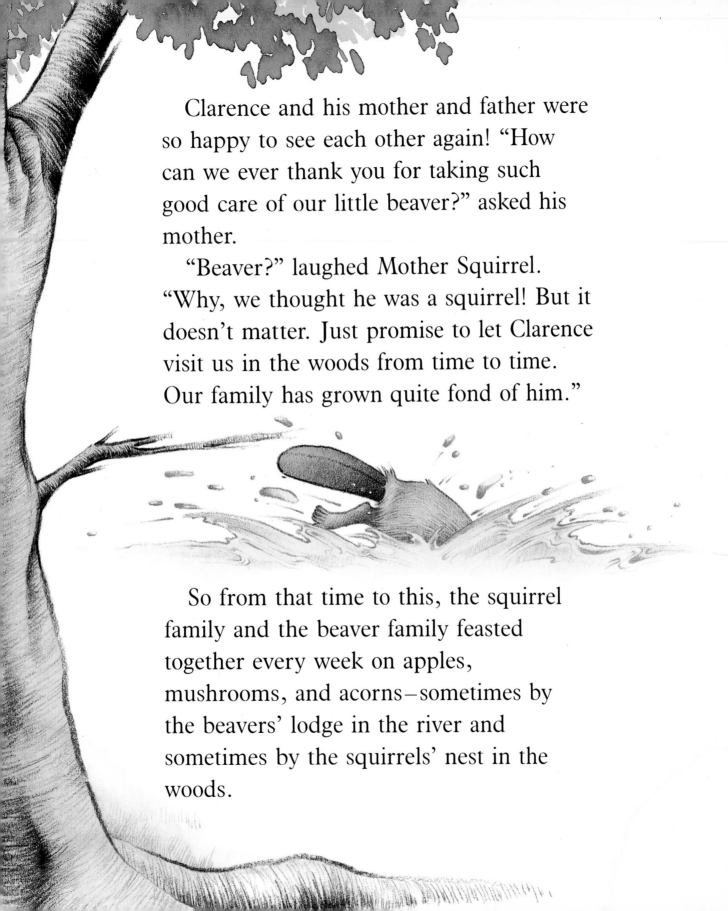

So from that time to this, the squirrel family and the beaver family feasted together every week on apples, mushrooms, and acorns—sometimes by the beavers' lodge in the river and sometimes by the squirrels' nest in the woods.

The beaver is the largest rodent in North America. Other rodents are squirrels, woodchucks, chipmunks, and mice. All rodents have sharp front teeth.

Beavers are good parents. Most beavers have two to four babies each year. Sometimes the mother beaver carries her little ones on her back when she swims!

Beavers are wonderful swimmers. They can stay under water for 15 minutes without coming up for air.